The Mannerly Adventures of Little Mouse by Martha Keenan

illustrated by Meri Shardin

Crown Publishers, Inc., New York

The text of this book is set in 14 point Bembo. The illustrations are three color pre-separated
pencil drawings.

Library of Congress Cataloging in Publication Data
Keenan, Martha.
    The mannerly adventures of Little Mouse.
    Summary: Though he tries hard, Little Mouse has
trouble remembering his manners.
    [1. Behavior—Fiction.   2. Mice—Fiction]
I. Shardin, Meri.   II. Title.
PZ7.K229Man3   [E]   76-41397
ISBN 0-517-528452

For Sue and Kathy

Little Mouse lived in a house tucked snugly under the floorboards of a very large kitchen. He lived there with Mama Mouse and Papa Mouse and his two sisters. Little Mouse was the youngest of them all.

One afternoon Mama Mouse called to her children to come in from a game of tag. "Uncle Cheddar is coming to help your father and me lay the pebbles for the floor in the new room. You know he will want to see you, so be sure to remember your manners," she said, helping them wash their paws. "Manners are very important." Then she gave each one a kiss and said, "I am proud of you."

"Even me?" asked Little Mouse.

"Of course," Mama Mouse said, giving him an extra kiss.

"But I always forget my manners," said Little Mouse. "I get mixed up."

Mama Mouse hugged him. "You are still very young. You will learn."

Just then there was a shuffling noise in the doorway. A large
sack appeared, followed by Uncle Cheddar. "Hello," he said.
"You're all looking well."

Little Mouse pointed to Uncle Cheddar's sack. "Are those presents for us?" he asked.

"Now, Little Mouse," said Mama Mouse, "if Uncle Cheddar has a present for you, he will offer it to you when he is ready."

"As a matter of fact," laughed Uncle Cheddar, "there are only pebbles in this sack. But I just happen to have something you might like in my pocket." He reached into his bulging jacket pocket and brought out three cheese crackers.

Little Mouse gobbled his cracker.

Mama Mouse bent down close to him. "Uncle Cheddar gave you something he thought you would like. Do you have something to say to him?"

"Yes," said Little Mouse. "May I have some more?"

His sisters giggled.

"You were supposed to say, 'Thank you,'" said Mama Mouse.

"I forgot," said Little Mouse.

His sisters took their crackers and said, "Thank you, Uncle Cheddar."

"You're welcome," said Uncle Cheddar.

Mama Mouse and Uncle Cheddar went off to help Papa Mouse in the new room.

"Let's play in the bedroom," said the oldest sister.

"Yes," said the other. "Let's play jacks."

"I would rather play marbles," said Little Mouse to himself. He pulled a bag of marbles from his pocket and arranged them on the kitchen floor. He could hear his parents and Uncle Cheddar working and his sisters laughing and singing a rhyme while they played jacks. Just when he was hoping to hit two marbles with one shot, his oldest sister called, "Mama! Mama! I've lost my cracker."

Mama Mouse and Little Mouse and Uncle Cheddar all hurried to the bedroom.

"Don't worry. I will help you find it," said Mama Mouse, as she looked on top of the dresser.

"I will help you, too," said the other sister, as she crawled among the books on the bookcase.

"I will help, too," said Little Mouse, as he sniffed his way across the bedroom floor and under the bed.

"Here it is! Here it is!" shouted Little Mouse, and he jumped up and down and popped the cracker into his mouth.

"He ate it!" screamed his sister. "Little Mouse ate my cracker!"

"That cracker was not yours, Little Mouse," Mama Mouse said. "What have you to say to your sister?"

Little Mouse bent down his head and tried to think. He thought and thought, but he did not know what to say.

"Surely there is something you want to say," said Mama
Mouse gently.

"Yes," said Little Mouse proudly. *"I found the cracker."*

"And you ate it!" cried his oldest sister.

"Your sister is very unhappy," scolded Mama Mouse.
"You should have told her you were sorry."

"I forgot," said Little Mouse sadly. "I'm sorry."

"Don't worry," said Uncle Cheddar. "Come with me. I have a few extra crackers, enough to make it all come out even." So the two sisters went with Uncle Cheddar, and Little Mouse picked up his marbles. Then he sat in a corner of the kitchen floor.

"From now on," he promised himself, "I will remember my manners." Then over and over he practiced the words. "I am sorry," he said. "Thank you," he said.

Mama Mouse and Uncle Cheddar found Little Mouse there later, still feeling sad.

"No need to be so unhappy," said Uncle Cheddar. "Maybe I can cheer you up. The people upstairs have had a barbecue. The patio is covered with crumbs. Do you want to go there with me?"

Little Mouse bent down his head, thinking, "What should I say, Mama? I don't know what to say."

"Do you want to go with your Uncle Cheddar?" Mama
Mouse asked.

"Oh, yes!" said Little Mouse.

Mama Mouse smiled. "Then say so. Say 'Yes, please.'"

"Yes, please! Yes, please!" said Little Mouse, jumping up and
down. He put on his jacket and took Uncle Cheddar's paw.
Together they crawled up the water pipe that led to the sink
in the very large kitchen, squeezed through the hole Papa
Mouse had made in the side of the house, and popped out into
the sunshine.

Once on the patio they found just what Uncle Cheddar had
promised—bits of cheese, hamburger, potato chips, sweet
pickles. Little Mouse scurried over the bricks, trying to decide
what would taste best. Uncle Cheddar, older and wiser and
always hungry, started eating at once. By the time Little Mouse
had finally picked up some cheese, Uncle Cheddar could not
fit one more French fried potato into his big, round belly.

"It is getting late," said Uncle Cheddar. "We should be going home."

"Wait!" said Little Mouse. "I see some corn."

Uncle Cheddar burped.

"Wait!" said Little Mouse. "I see some celery."

Uncle Cheddar yawned.

"Wait!" said Little Mouse. "I see some lettuce. And a marshmallow. And a chocolate chip cookie."

Uncle Cheddar felt very full and very sleepy. "We must go home," he said, and he motioned to Little Mouse to follow.

Little Mouse saw one whole olive under the barbecue table.
He ran to get it. Then he turned around to follow Uncle
Cheddar, but Uncle Cheddar was gone. Little Mouse found his
way home alone.

Mama and Papa Mouse were angry.

"You know better than to stay out alone," said Mama Mouse, tapping her foot. "While you have been thinking only of yourself, your father and I have been very worried. We were just going to look for you."

"That's right," said Papa Mouse. "I think a spanking is in order. Don't you?"

Little Mouse was so tired, all he could remember was his Mama's last lesson in manners. "Yes, please," he said wearily.

Papa Mouse chuckled.

Then Little Mouse realized what he had said. "No! No! I don't want to be spanked! I'm late because I wanted to bring home a surprise."

And with that Little Mouse sighed so deeply that the bottom
button of his jacket popped open. Pop! Pop! Pop! One by one
the buttons burst open and the bits of cheese, corn, celery,
and lettuce leaves he had collected fell to the floor. The whole
olive rolled to a stop between Papa's legs.

Little Mouse pulled a marshmallow from his pocket and
handed it to Mama Mouse. "Everything looked so good. I tried
to bring it *all* home so everyone could have some. I'm sorry."

Papa Mouse hugged his son. "There's nothing to be sorry about, Little Mouse," he said. "I am proud of you."

"Yes," agreed Mama Mouse. "You have showed the truest manners of all. Thank you, Little Mouse."

Little Mouse bent down his head. A small thought formed in his mind. He wasn't sure it was right, but he tried it anyway. "You're welcome," he said softly.

Mama Mouse smiled at him, so he said it again. *"You're welcome."*

Then Little Mouse grinned from ear to ear, for he knew he had said—and done—exactly what was right.

DATE			